I Had a Bad Dream

A Book About Nightmares

By Linda Hayward
Illustrated by Eugenie

*Prepared with the cooperation of Bernice Berk, Ph.D.,
of the Bank Street College of Education*

A GOLDEN BOOK · NEW YORK

Western Publishing Company, Inc., Racine, Wisconsin 53404

Note to Parents

The story and pictures in this book describe an expe-
rience that may be familiar to young listeners, for it is
natural for children to have bad dreams. Nightmares may
come from a variety of sources in the child's world, and
these cannot easily be controlled by parents. But parents
can comfort and soothe children when they are
frightened by a dream, and help them to separate reality
from fantasy.

In this story, Jason's nightmare is triggered by his
unhappiness at having to stop his bathtime play and get
ready for bed. Elements of the real world crop up in his
dream—the giant who Jason later thinks is in the bathtub;
the little brother whom Jason must rescue. Thus Jason's
father is able to "check out" the content of the dream
with Jason. Together they discover that only boats are in
the tub; and together they find Jason's brother fast asleep
in his own bed. Now Jason can separate his nightmare
from the safety of the real world.

When the content of your child's bad dream bears
resemblance to reality, it can be helpful to check it out in
this way. Your goal is to dispel any lingering anxiety or
confusion the child may feel about whether the dream
really happened. Reading this book with your child can
allay the fears associated with nightmares, and lead to
easy, open discussion of them.

—The Editors

Jason's brother was afraid of the dark.
Not Jason!

Jason's brother was afraid of the big dog
behind the tall fence.

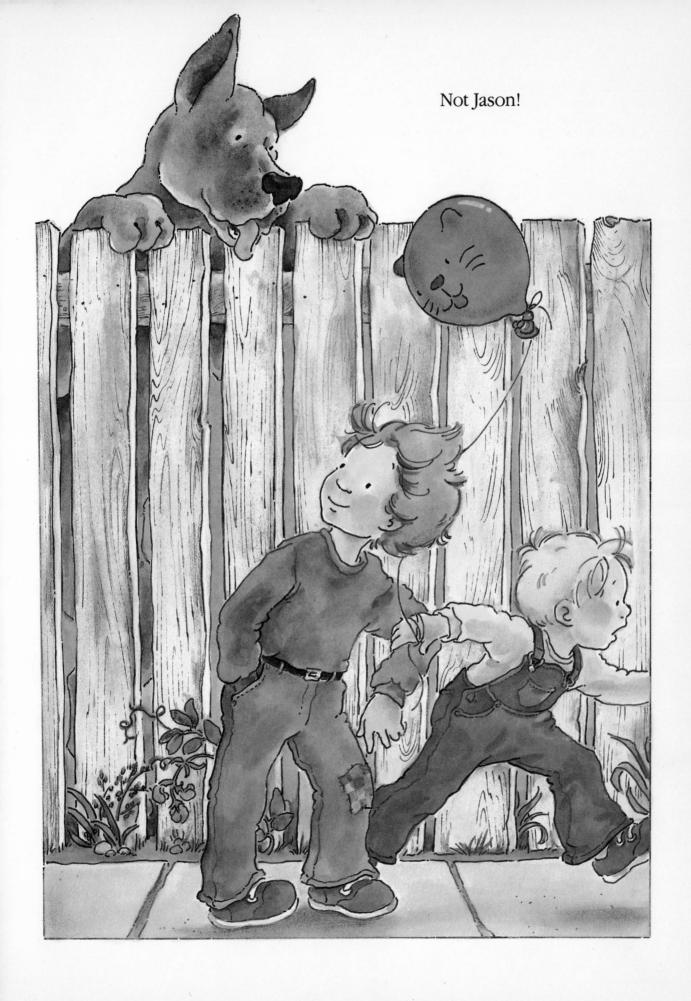

Not Jason!

Sometimes Jason's brother was afraid to go
in the wading pool.

Not Jason!
He was teaching his brother how to have fun
in the water.

Jason loved the water.
When he took a bath, he always had a good time.
One night he was in charge of all the ships at sea—a
tanker, a freighter, three sailboats, and a steamer full of
passengers.

Jason scooted back and forth in the water.
He made the waves that rocked the boats.
The waves sloshed and splashed over the edge
of the tub.

The steamer started to sink.
The passengers needed his help.
Just then Jason's father appeared in the doorway.
He looked very tall.

"Jason!" he said in a stern voice. "Stop that splashing!
The floor is covered with water. It's time for you to get
out."

Jason had to get out of the bathtub.

He felt bad that he could not rescue his passengers.

When Jason was in bed, his father read him a story. It was a story about a hero named Jason, who sailed on a boat called the *Argo*.

Jason fell asleep.

In the middle of the night, Jason had a dream.
He dreamed his brother was drowning.
Jason was the only one who could rescue him.

To reach his brother, Jason first had to go through a dark, scary place.
Jason was brave.

He had to walk past a big, scary dog.
For Jason, that was easy.

Then he had to step into the water without waking up
a sleeping giant.
Jason moved very quietly.
But when he stepped into the water, his foot made
a splash.
The splash woke up the sleeping giant.

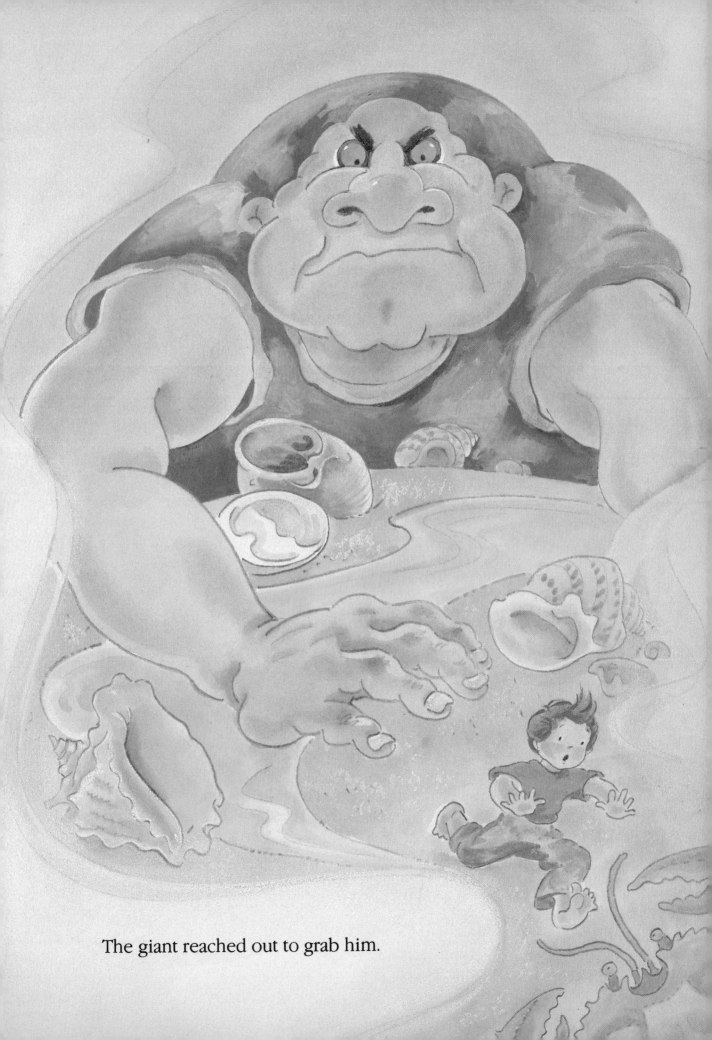

The giant reached out to grab him.

Jason woke up.

He felt afraid and he did not know why.

Then he remembered his dream about
the sleeping giant.

Jason went and woke up his father.
"I had a bad dream," he said.

Jason's father put his arms around Jason.
Jason began to feel safe again.

They went to look at Jason's brother.
He was fast asleep in his own bed.
"It was just a dream," said Jason.

"Now where is that sleeping giant?" said his father.
Jason thought of a place.
"In the bathtub," he said.

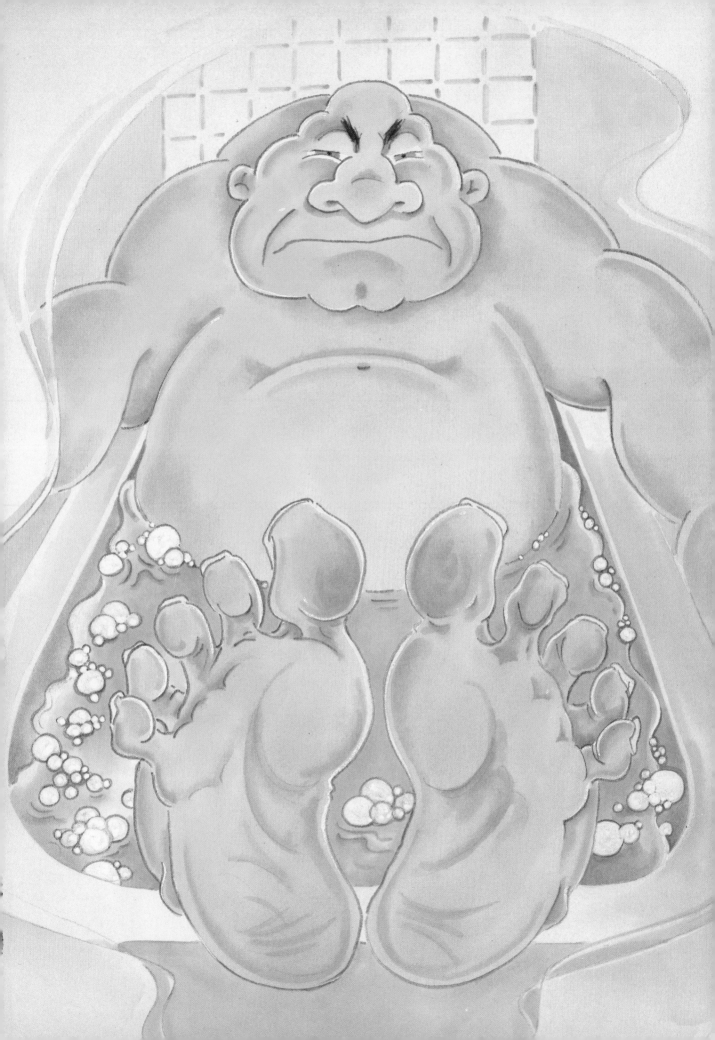

But there were only boats in the bathtub.
The sleeping giant wasn't there.
"It was just a dream," said Jason.

He put the passengers back into the steamer and set it
on the shelf.
Then he went back to bed.
Was Jason afraid to go to sleep?